Stable Boy at the Alamo

Monitor vs. Merrimack: Clash of the Ironclads

Two Historical Fiction Stories About Famous Battles from 19th-Century U.S. History

by Angelo Parra
illustrated by Martin Hargreaves

Table of Contents

HISTORICAL FICTION

What is historical fiction?

Historical fiction stories take place in the past. Historical fiction stories have characters, settings, and events based on historical facts. The characters can be based on real people or made up. The dialogue is made up. But the information about the time period must be authentic, or factually accurate. The stories explore a conflict, or problem, that characters have with themselves, with other characters, or with nature.

What is the purpose of historical fiction?

Historical fiction blends history and fiction into stories that could have actually happened. It adds a human element to history. Readers can learn about the time period: how people lived, what they owned, and even what they ate and wore. Readers can also see how people's problems and feelings have not changed much over time. In addition, historical fiction entertains you as you "escape" into adventures from the past.

How do you read historical fiction?

The title gives you a clue about an important time, place, character, or situation. As you read, note how the characters' lives are the same as and different from people's lives today. Note the main characters' thoughts, feelings, and actions. How do they change from the beginning of the story to the end? Ask yourself, *What moves this character to take action? What can I learn today from his or her struggles long ago?*

Features of Historical Fiction

The characters lived or could have lived in the time and place portrayed.

The story takes place in an authentic historical setting.

The events did occur or could have occurred in the setting.

The dialogue is made up but may be based on letters, a diary, or a report.

At least one character deals with a conflict (self, others, or nature).

The story is told from a first-person or third-person point of view.

Who tells the story in historical fiction?

Authors usually write historical fiction in one of two ways. In the first-person point of view, one of the characters tells the story as it happens to him or her, using words such as **I**, **me**, **my**, **mine**, **we**, **us**, and **our**. In the third-person point of view, a narrator tells the story and refers to the characters using words such as **he**, **him**, and **his**; **she**, **her**, and **hers**; and **their**. The narrator may also refer to the characters by name, for example, "Will grinned and blushed."

TOOLS FOR READERS AND WRITERS

A Strong Lead

A strong lead, or first few sentences, grabs or hooks readers. A strong lead makes readers want to keep reading. The lead tells you something important about the topic or main character and hints at what might happen. Authors use two types of leads. A direct lead tells who or what the story is about. An indirect lead may describe a setting, tell an anecdote, or true story, about the main character or topic, or ask a question.

Easily Confused Words

Many words in the English language are used incorrectly because they are confusing. They may sound or be spelled similarly, which often leads to their being used interchangeably—and incorrectly. **Cease**, which means "stop," and **seize**, which means "to grasp," are examples. Good readers will reread passages with easily confused words so that they understand the writer's intended meaning. Good writers reread what they have written to make sure they have used these easily confused words in their writing correctly.

Make Inferences

Good authors don't explain everything in a story. Often, authors provide clues and evidence in their stories and expect the reader to "read between the lines," or make inferences. Good readers consider the information an author provides and think about other truths it suggests. To make an inference, look for parts of the text that make you stop and think to yourself, *I wonder if the author is saying that . . .*

The Battle of the Alamo

The historic Battle of the Alamo took place in what is today the city of San Antonio, Texas. Famous pioneers and frontiersmen Jim Bowie and Davy Crockett fought in the famous battle. This heroic and tragic fight was an important part of the Texas War of Independence and the history of the United States.

In the 1820s, the territory that's now the state of Texas belonged to Mexico. Thousands of Americans were allowed to move into the territory to establish farms and ranches, becoming "Texians." Soon Texians far outnumbered the Mexicans there.

In 1830, the Mexican government decided to stop further settlement by outsiders. Mexico also increased taxes on the Texians and tried to outlaw slavery in the territory. Texians rejected these changes, and fighting broke out.

In 1836, Mexican general Antonio López de Santa Anna led an army against a band of about 200 Texians, headed by Bowie, Crockett, and William B. Travis. The Texians were barricaded in an enclosed, fort-like church and grounds, known as the Alamo.

Santa Anna's army surrounded the Alamo. After thirteen days of fighting, Santa Anna's army of 1,500 soldiers stormed the walls of the Alamo, overwhelming and defeating the Texians. Though the Texians suffered a terrible loss that day, their heroism inspired the battle cry: "Remember the Alamo!" Those words encouraged other Texians to continue and win the fight for independence from Mexico.

The Battle of the *Monitor* and the *Merrimack*

The Battle of the *Monitor* and the *Merrimack* is the most famous naval battle of the Civil War. It was a historic clash between two new kinds of warships called ironclads (wooden ships covered with iron), one from the North and one from the South.

The battle between the Union Navy's *Monitor* and the Confederate Navy's *Merrimack* took place in the waters between Virginia's James River and Chesapeake Bay. It began as part of an effort by the Confederacy to break a Union blockade that cut off Virginia's largest cities, Norfolk and Richmond, from foreign trade and supplies.

On March 8, 1862, the South's *Merrimack* attacked the Union blockade. It sank two Union ships and seriously damaged another. The next day, the North's *Monitor* arrived and the two warships exchanged cannon fire for three hours.

In this first battle of ironclads ships, there was no winner and no loser, and surprisingly little damage. But the age of wooden fighting ships was coming to an end. The era of iron and steel battleships had begun.

An ironclad had no masts or sails. Instead, it moved through the water with an underwater propeller powered by a coal-fired steam engine inside the ship. Cannonballs bounced off the sides of ironclad warships.

Stable Boy at the Alamo

For the past twelve days about two hundred of us had been trapped inside the fort. I heard Colonel Bill Travis say there were many hundreds, maybe thousands, of Mexican soldiers camped outside our walls. The army of the Mexican general Santa Anna had the fort, and us, surrounded. Our storerooms were nearly bare.

Earlier, cannonballs had knocked down some of the fort's inner buildings and put cracks in the walls. A messenger from Santa Anna offered us the chance to surrender. A cannonball fired into the Mexican lines was our response.

The photo above shows the restored facade of the Alamo, lit up at night.

I couldn't sleep so I took a walk around the fort. It must have been around four in the morning, and it was cold. March nights in the Texas territory can be chilly. I pulled my coat tightly closed around me.

I walked along the fortified walls of the fort, looking out at the distant campfires of the Mexican army. There were so many fires glowing in the darkness that it looked like we were in the center of a ring of fire. I said hello to the sentries keeping watch as I passed.

"What keeps a young fella like you awake?" asked one of the guards. "You scared?"

"No, sir," I lied.

"What's your name, boy?" he asked with a smile I could barely see in the dark.

"Harold, sir," I told him.

"My name is Jeremiah," said the guard as he put down his rifle and took out a pipe. "This here Alamo ain't a bad place to be, Harold."

Map labels: N, W, E, S; UNITED STATES; Santa Fe; MEXICO; DISPUTED TERRITORY; El Paso; REPUBLIC OF TEXAS; The Alamo; The Battle of San Jacinto; San Antonio; Rio Grande; Gulf of Mexico; 0 200 mi

Legend:
- U.S. state border
- Border claimed by Mexico in 1836
- Border claimed by Texas in 1836
- Republic of Texas (1836-1845)

Jeremiah told me that the Alamo started out as a church. Around 1800, the site was converted into a fort. Barracks were added for soldiers to sleep in. High, two-foot-thick walls were built with adobe brick for protection and to hold cannons, about twenty of them, for defense.

"How old are you?" he asked.

"Sixteen," I lied.

"You look more like twelve to me," Jeremiah said with a chuckle.

"Thirteen," I stated, correcting him truthfully. "I'm just the stable boy. But I can handle a gun!"

"Caring for horses, now that's important work," he said, blowing smoke rings. The pipe seemed to have a calming **effect** on him. "There's plenty of ways to fight for independence without going around shooting off one of these."

Jeremiah picked up his rifle and again looked out into the darkness toward the Mexican army. His smile disappeared. "Take care, young fella," he said without taking his eyes off the distant fires.

I **proceeded** along the walls of the Alamo. After a few minutes, I heard men in conversation and recognized the voices. They

In this illustration, Colonel William Travis (left) is mustering his men, including Davy Crockett.

belonged to Bill Travis, our commander, and Davy Crockett, the famous frontiersman from Tennessee.

"There are sounds of movement coming from the Mexican camps," Crockett said. "At this hour of the early morning it should be quiet."

"The Mexicans are up to something," Travis agreed. He turned in my direction, saw me, and said sharply, "Who's there?"

"Harold, the stable boy," I answered quickly.

Travis and Crockett returned their attention to the Mexican camps.

"A full attack could come today," Crockett said to Colonel Travis.

Suddenly, Colonel Travis turned toward me again. "Son, I need you to take a message to Colonel Bowie."

Surprised, I could only nod in agreement.

"Run over to Colonel Bowie's quarters, and tell him we're seeing activity in the Mexican lines."

"Yes, sir!" I said enthusiastically, running off in the direction of the barracks. Everybody knew that Colonel Jim Bowie was very sick. The doctor had ordered him to remain in his room.

I knocked on Colonel Bowie's door and entered. The colonel was in his bed.

"What is it, boy?" Bowie asked, propping himself up on an elbow.

I gave him the message about the possible attack. The news seemed to **affect** him deeply.

"I wish there was something I could do about it," he said, sinking back onto the bed.

When I got back to Colonel Travis and Davy Crockett, I found them talking quietly with another man.

"If you go now, in the dark, you might be able to sneak past the Mexican camps," Crockett was saying.

"Get the message out that we need help," Travis added. "Good luck!"

"I'll do my best, Colonel," the man responded.

"And take this young man with you," Crockett added. "There's no reason for him to stay here in danger."

I followed the man back to the stable, and I brought out his horse. The man threw his saddle onto the horse's back and climbed up. He held his hand out to me. "Get on up here, boy," he said. "Hurry!"

"No, thank you, sir," I responded.

"You were told to come with me," he said, citing Crockett's order.

"My place is here," I asserted, backing away from him.

"Suit yourself," he said with a shrug. He could see that he would never be able to **persuade** me to leave the fort.

The gate to the Alamo was opened quietly, and the man slowly rode out into the darkness.

The sun was beginning to rise and the sky **lightening** as I reported to Colonel Travis and Davy Crockett that the man was on his way.

"I thought you were told to go with him," Colonel Travis said to me angrily.

"I want to help fight, sir," I said. "I'm a Texian, too!"

Before Colonel Travis could respond, the sound of gunshots woke the dawn earlier than usual.

"Round up the women and children, son!" Colonel Travis said, speaking rapidly. "Take them into the back room of the barracks, lock the door, and stay with them. That's an order."

I turned and dashed across the open courtyard of the fort toward the barracks. Men were shouting, grabbing their weapons, and running to their places on the walls. They were **convinced** the main attack had begun. Cannons began firing, flashing like **lightning** and booming like thunder.

There weren't many civilians in the fort, just a few wives and children of some of the men. I led about a dozen people into the back room of the barracks. Before locking the door, I ran to Colonel Bowie's room to tell him the fighting had started.

"Hand me those guns," Colonel Bowie said, pointing to a pair of pistols on a table. Beside the guns was a big curved hunting knife. I quickly handed the guns to him.

"See my knife, boy? Take it," Colonel Bowie said. "Won't do me much good in bed."

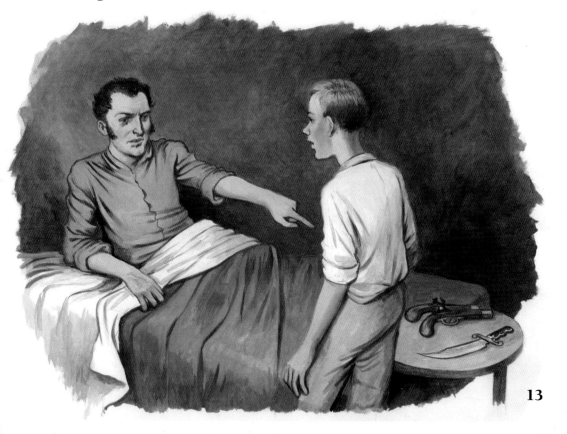

I picked up the handsome knife, thanked the colonel, and hurried back to the room with the women and children. I stepped inside, locked the door, and pushed a table and some chairs against it.

It was quiet in the room as we listened to the gunfire and rumble of artillery. The battle went on for hours. The women cowered at the sound of the cannon blasts and some of the children cried. I stood between them and the door, grasping Bowie's knife.

Eventually, the noises stopped. The battle was over. We couldn't tell who had won. Then we heard shouting outside the room, and someone began pounding on our door. The pounding became a resounding crash; the door burst open, sending the chairs and table flying. Three soldiers in blue and red coats with white pants and blue caps rushed in, carrying rifles. Mexicans!

The Alamo was lost.

Amid the shrieks and cries I held my knife out, ready to fight. "Stand back!" I told the women and children. The soldiers said something in Spanish. One of them left while two held us at gunpoint. A minute later, a man in a regal uniform strode into the room. He glanced at the scene around him, then looked directly at me and pulled up a chair. He sat, weary, but still erect.

"I am Antonio López de Santa Anna," he said to me in English. "My men, they tell me they want to shoot you. I wonder if I should let them. What is your name?"

"Harold Evans," I answered, keeping an eye on the soldiers and their rifles.

"You are holding a beautiful knife, Mr. Evans. May I see it? I promise I will give it back to you."

Here was my chance! I could kill Santa Anna. I would be a hero! But . . . if I attacked him, there would be shooting throughout the room. That would endanger the women and children. My job was to protect them.

I handed the knife to the general. "It's Jim Bowie's knife," I pointed out proudly. "He gave it to me."

Santa Anna looked at it closely, feeling its weight in his hand.

"Ah, yes, Señor Bowie's famous knife. Magnificent," he said, giving the knife back to me. "It is yours now. You are a brave young man, Señor Evans. You have acted wisely. I will give the order that you and these people may leave the fort safely."

The general stood, nodded his head toward me, and left the room.

Minutes later, the soldiers put us in horse-drawn wagons. My wagon **preceded** the group as we went through the gates of the Alamo. I tried not to look at the bodies of the hundreds of men—Texians and Mexicans—on the walls and around the fort. Instead, I looked down at the Bowie knife, secure in my belt, that I had not used in my fight for independence.

Analyze the Characters, Setting, and Plot

- Who are the characters in this story?
- What is the setting for this story?
- Why is Jim Bowie in bed?
- Davy Crockett tells Harold to go with the messenger. Harold does not go. Why does he want to stay at the Alamo?
- Jim Bowie cannot get out of bed, yet he asks Harold for his guns as if he is going to fight. What does he intend to do with his guns?
- What happens at the end of the story?

Focus on Comprehension: Make Inferences

- No one has been able to get food inside the fort. How can you tell?
- Jeremiah says that there are plenty of ways to fight for independence without going around shooting guns. What does that tell you about Jeremiah?
- Jim Bowie's knife is known by everyone. How can you tell?

Focus on Story: Mood

Authors develop a story's mood by including characters, details, and events that lead readers to feel certain emotions throughout the story. Story moods include fear, intrigue, euphoria, contentment, and nostalgia. This historical fiction story's mood suggests that something bad is going to happen. Identify three events that make you feel as if something bad might happen.

Analyze the Tools Writers Use: A Strong Lead

Look at the lead in this story.
- What type of lead does the author use in this story?
- Did the lead hook you as a reader? Why?
- What did you expect to learn after reading the lead?

Focus on Words: Easily Confused Words

Make a chart like the one below. Locate the easily confused words in the story. Read the sentence containing each word and the sentences around it. Then write a definition for the word.

Page	Word	Definition
10	effect	
11	affect	
10	proceeded	
15	preceded	
12	persuade	
13	convinced	
12	lightening	
13	lightning	

Monitor vs. Merrimack:
Clash of the Ironclads

Will Randall stood on the deck of a strange boat, bundled up against the frigid winter air blowing off the icy water of New York Harbor. The tall, light-haired young man wore a heavy navy blue coat and thick woolen gloves, **complemented** by a naval cap. But the freezing, raw February weather could not dampen his enthusiasm and excitement. He was a first-time sailor on the newest, most up-to-date ship in the Union Navy.

The ship, an ironclad named the *Monitor*, had just departed from the Brooklyn Navy Yard.

The vessel and its crew of more than fifty seamen were heading into enemy waters, in Virginia. When they arrived at Hampton Roads Harbor, the *Monitor* would take on ships of the Confederate States of America.

Will was proud to be a crewman on the *Monitor*. Cannonballs would just bounce off the iron-covered sides of this modern warship. As a gunner, he was looking forward to firing one of the ship's two very big guns.

But the enthusiasm Will and his crewmates were feeling quickly turned to frustration. This was the *Monitor*'s maiden voyage and a mechanical problem appeared. The ship's helmsman discovered that the steering wasn't working well. It was stiff, making it very difficult to turn the ship.

A frustrated John Worden, the bearded captain of the *Monitor*, gave the order to return to port. Will and his fellow sailors were disappointed the *Monitor* hadn't gotten any **farther** than New York Harbor. People on shore laughed at the funny-looking, pancake-flat boat being towed back to the navy yard for repairs.

Hundreds of miles to the south, the navy of the Confederate States of America was completing an iron-covered ship of its own. Eli Reynolds, a dark-haired and muscular sailor, was helping to put the finishing touches on the South's first ironclad.

The author's mention of "Confederate States of America" establishes the story's historical setting as the period of the Civil War. The author also introduces the story's conflict: a Civil War naval battle.

The author is detailing an event in the "life" of the *Monitor*. The dates and events reflect actual history. Note that the author is using a third-person narrator to tell the story.

Readers are introduced to Eli, Will's counterpart on the *Merrimack*, and learn that he is as determined to win the battle for the South as Will is for the North.

Eli was eager to get the new warship into action. Union ships had set up a blockade of the Virginian coastline, preventing supplies from getting through. The Confederate ship was going to break up the blockade.

We'll teach those Yankees a lesson, Eli thought, as he helped push and fasten into place one of the ship's many big guns.

The author describes key events of the actual naval battle and advances the plot of the story.

Following repairs and a two-day journey, the *Monitor* arrived at Virginia late on Saturday as the sky grew dark. Bad news awaited Captain Worden. That very day the *Merrimack* had attacked Union ships blockading the Virginian coastline. Using its ram and guns, the *Merrimack* had destroyed and set aflame two Union warships. It also seriously damaged a third ship, the *Minnesota*.

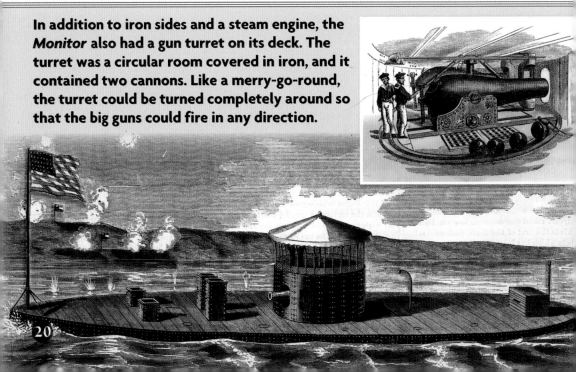

In addition to iron sides and a steam engine, the *Monitor* also had a gun turret on its deck. The turret was a circular room covered in iron, and it contained two cannons. Like a merry-go-round, the turret could be turned completely around so that the big guns could fire in any direction.

Hundreds of Union sailors lost their lives in that battle. Only the approaching darkness of night had stopped the *Merrimack* from doing more damage. In the distance, Captain Worden could see the smoke and red glow of the burning Union ships. He knew that if the *Merrimack* wasn't stopped, the next day it would attack and sink more Union vessels.

That evening, Captain Worden called the entire crew onto the deck of the *Monitor*. He pointed to the distant flames lighting up the night sky and told his men about the *Merrimack's* victory and the terrible loss of Union sailors and boats. He also said that the *Monitor* had just received orders to sail up to Washington, D.C., so that government officials could inspect the new ship.

"We have a choice, men," Captain Worden announced. "We can sail away to Washington to show off our boat, as instructed, or we can stay here and fight the *Merrimack* in the morning. We're all new to the *Monitor* and still learning the ropes. **Further**, for most of you, this would be your first naval combat.

The South's ironclad was built using the bottom portion and steam engines of a Union ship, the *Merrimack*, which had been sunk in the harbor at Norfolk, Virginia. A new deck was put atop the *Merrimack's* hull, on which workers erected a huge, long cabin that would hold the ship's guns, including ten cannons, five on each side. To make the *Merrimack* deadlier, Confederate shipbuilders added a ram, a large, heavy point of iron, at the front of the ship. The ram would be used to poke large holes in enemy vessels to sink them. The new Confederate ironclad was given a new name, the *Virginia*, but most people still called the boat the *Merrimack*.

When the fighting begins, we'd run the risk of **floundering**," he explained. "In other words, men, we can't be sure we will win a fight with the *Merrimack*. So what do you think we ought to do? Should we follow our orders and leave here, or stay and fight?"

The officers and crew of the *Monitor* numbered more than fifty, but not one said a thing or offered an opinion. A cool breeze flapped the uniforms of the men as they stood in an uneasy silence. After a few long minutes, Will Randall spoke up.

In this exchange of dialogue, the author reveals more about Will's character: he is determined to fight!

"Captain, we didn't come all this way to turn around just when things get tough," he said. "I believe in the *Monitor* and I believe in the Union, and I say let's show those Rebels what *our* ironclad can do!"

The crew erupted into a great cheer in unison. Captain Worden gladly shook Will's hand. The rest of the men crowded around Will, thanking him and slapping him on the back. Will grinned and blushed. He was not used to being **complimented**.

A courageous decision had been made. The *Monitor* would stay and do battle to stop the destruction being caused by the Confederate ironclad.

At dawn on the morning of March 9, 1862, the *Merrimack* sailed out of Norfolk harbor again to attack and destroy more of the Union fleet. Eli Reynolds peered out through one of the warship's gun ports to see which Union ship Captain Catesby Jones would choose as the next victim of the *Merrimack*.

> The author provides the exact date of the historical event on which the story is based.

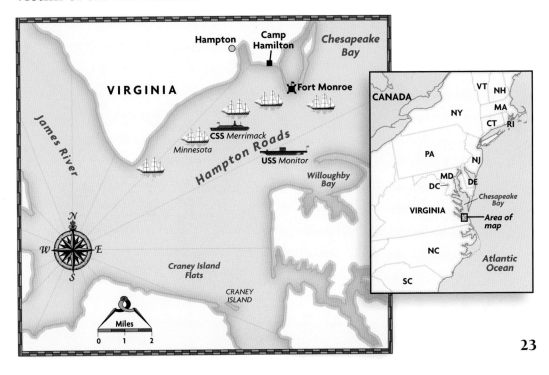

23

"Nobody can touch us," he said to himself. "Today, we'll finish the job we started yesterday."

Eli prepared to fire his cannon as the *Merrimack* approached its target, the damaged, unmoving *Minnesota*. She was a sitting duck.

To his surprise, Eli spotted a strange, flat, metal-covered boat coming out from behind the *Minnesota*. Another ironclad! Eli ran to the *Merrimack's* captain to give him the news of the approaching vessel.

"I've never seen anything like it," Eli said. "It looks like a tin can on a metal raft."

"That must be the *Monitor* we've been hearing about," Captain Jones replied. "Well, Seaman Reynolds, it looks like we're in for a battle. Get back to your gun."

Eli aimed his cannon at the *Monitor* and fired. The shot missed, kicking up a big splash of water. The turret of the *Monitor* turned toward the *Merrimack*. Inside, Will Randall fired one of the two turret cannons. The eleven-inch-wide cannonball hit the *Merrimack* hard on the side. Union sailors aboard the **foundering** *Minnesota* cheered.

The *Monitor's* cannonball did not break through the protective iron plating of the *Merrimack*, but the loud bang and vibration caused Eli's nose to bleed. Eli wiped his bloody nose with his sleeve. There was no time to stop.

Captain Jones ordered the *Merrimack's* helmsman to turn the warship's side toward the *Monitor*, enabling the *Merrimack* to fire broadside from all the guns on one side of the ship. The *Merrimack* fired. The multiple shots dented the armor of the *Monitor* and rattled Will's teeth. But no serious harm had been done.

Like two prizefighters in a boxing match, the two ironclads circled each other, firing away. The *Monitor*, smaller than the *Merrimack*, was a bit quicker. Cannonballs rocketed and ricocheted off each ship. Clouds of gunpowder smoke surrounded the battling boats, making it hard for the crew of the *Minnesota* and the spectators on land to see what was happening.

The author further develops the plot by describing an action-packed battle that will keep readers engaged. This is the crisis, or turning point, of the story.

The author is using a technique called parallel structure. He puts both main characters into a difficult situation, but each emerges with only minor wounds. Readers see that Will and Eli are really not so different from each other.

After hours of exchanging shots, the *Merrimack*'s captain decided to try ramming the *Monitor*. His helmsman aimed the front of the *Merrimack* at the *Monitor*. "Full speed!" Captain Jones ordered.

Because the *Monitor* was faster, Captain Worden managed to move his ship out of the path of the *Merrimack*, which struck the *Monitor* only a glancing blow. The *Monitor* suffered no damage, but, ironically, the minimal contact caused the *Merrimack* to spring a leak. The Confederate ironclad began taking on water. In need of repairs after three hours of artillery give and take, the *Merrimack* had to break off the fight.

This 1889 lithograph of the battle between the *Monitor* and *Merrimack* is by Kurz & Allison, a printing company known for depicting dramatic scenes from American history.

As the *Merrimack* sailed away, Eli, his shirt covered with blood, sweat, and gunpowder soot, fired one last time at the *Monitor*, which was following the *Merrimack*.

"Right into the pilot house!" he cried. "Wahoo!"

The *Merrimack's* blast wounded the *Monitor's* captain. Will rushed to kneel beside his fallen commander. As Will helped Captain Worden to the ship's medic for treatment, the captain ordered the *Monitor* to give up its pursuit of the *Merrimack*. The battle was now over as both ships headed off for repair.

Will Randall stepped into the damaged pilothouse and looked out the view hole. He watched the *Merrimack* move toward port. Both crews had fought courageously. This was the end of today's battle, Will knew, but the beginning of a new kind of naval warfare.

As Will observed the retreating *Merrimack*, he thought he saw, for a moment, a young, dark-haired sailor on the Confederate ironclad salute him. Will stood up tall and saluted back.

Analyze the Characters, Setting, and Plot

- Who are the characters in this story?
- What is the setting for this story?
- What is the name of the Union ironclad? What is the name of the Confederate ironclad?
- What are the ironclads capable of doing?
- What is the problem with the *Monitor*? What did the sailors decide to do about the problem?
- The *Merrimack* captain decides to ram the *Monitor*. Why?
- What happens at the end of the story?

Focus on Comprehension: Make Inferences

- The author says that "cannonballs would just bounce off the iron-covered sides of this modern warship." What can you infer about the *Monitor* from this sentence?
- The *Merrimack* cannot do battle at night. How can you tell?
- The two young sailors on the ironclad have a mutual respect for each other. How can you tell?

Analyze the Tools Writers Use: A Strong Lead

Look at the lead in this story.
- What type of lead does the author use in this story?
- Did the lead hook you as a reader? Why?
- What did you expect to learn after reading the lead?

Focus on Words: Easily Confused Words

Make a chart like the one below. Locate the easily confused word in the story. Read the sentence containing each word and the sentences around it. Then write a definition for the word.

Page	Word	Definition
18	complemented	
23	complimented	
19	farther	
21	further	
22	floundering	
25	foundering	

This photo of the crew of the *Monitor* was taken on the James River, Virginia, by noted photographer Mathew Brady.

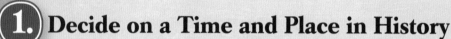

THE WRITER'S CRAFT

How does an author write HISTORICAL FICTION?

Reread "*Monitor* vs. *Merrimack*: Clash of the Ironclads" and think about what Angelo Parra did to write this story. How did he develop the story? How can you, as a writer, develop your own historical fiction story?

1. Decide on a Time and Place in History

a. Choose a time 30 years ago, 3,000 years ago, or somewhere in between. Set your story in your home country or far away.

b. Learn everything you can about the lives of people who lived in that time and place so your story details will be authentic. In "*Monitor* vs. *Merrimack*: Clash of the Ironclads," the author researched the Civil War battle between the first Union and Confederate ironclad warships.

c. Choose an actual event to rewrite into your own historical fiction story, or create a story based on the life of a historical figure.

Character	Will Randall	Eli Reynolds
Traits	excited; brave	confident; determined
Examples	excited to be a crewman standing on the deck of the Union's first ironclad warship; he shows his bravery in his desire to stay and fight the *Merrimack* instead of going to Washington to show off the *Monitor*	sure that the *Merrimack* will "teach those Yankees a lesson"; doesn't let a bloody nose stop him from doing his job in the heat of battle

2. Brainstorm Characters

Writers ask these questions:

- What kind of person will my main character be? What are his or her traits, or qualities?
- What is important to my main character? What does he or she want?
- What other characters will be important to my story? How will each character help or hinder the main character?
- How will the characters change? What will they learn about life?

3. Brainstorm Plot

Writers ask these questions:

- What are some important incidents that actually occurred in my historical setting? How can I turn one of those real-life experiences into a story?
- What is the problem, or situation?
- What events happen?
- How does the story end?
- Will my readers be entertained? Will they learn something?

Setting	Aboard the Union Navy's *Monitor* and the Confederate Navy's *Merrimack* in the waters between Virginia's James River and Chesapeake Bay, 1862.
Problem of the Story	The Confederacy is determined to break a Union blockade of ships that are cutting off Virginia's largest cities, Norfolk and Richmond, from foreign trade and supplies.
Story Events	1. The Union's *Monitor* has to return to the Brooklyn Navy Yard for repairs to its steering before it heads into battle at Hampton Roads Harbor in Virginia. 2. The Confederacy's *Merrimack* attacks Union ships that are part of the blockade, damaging several and destroying two. 3. The *Monitor* enters the fray instead of going to Washington to be shown to government officials. 4. The *Monitor* and the *Merrimack* do battle, during which the *Merrimack* springs a leak. 5. As the *Merrimack* retreats for repairs, it manages to inflict damage on the *Monitor*.
Solution to the Problem	The clash of the ironclads resulted in a draw. It became known as the most famous naval battle of the Civil War.

Glossary

affect   (uh-FEKT) produce an emotional reaction in someone (page 11)

complemented   (KAHM-plih-men-ted) completed or perfected, as in a coordinating part of something, like clothing (page 18)

complimented   (KAHM-plih-men-ted) honored or praised with remarks or gestures of admiration or esteem (page 23)

convinced   (kun-VINST) led by strong evidence or argument to believe in something and possibly to act (page 13)

effect   (ih-FEKT) an influence or reaction produced by someone or something (page 10)

farther   (FAR-ther) to a greater distance or more advanced point (page 19)

floundering   (FLOWN-duh-ring) struggling clumsily; failing to establish solid footing in order to make progress (page 22)

foundering   (FOWN-duh-ring) sinking below the water's surface (page 25)

further   (FER-ther) moreover; in addition (page 21)

lightening   (LY-teh-ning) growing brighter; less dark (page 12)

lightning   (LITE-ning) electrical discharge in the sky during a storm (page 13)

persuade   (per-SWADE) convince through argument, encouragement, or pleading to agree or take action (page 12)

preceded   (prih-SEE-ded) was positioned ahead of or happened earlier than something (page 15)

proceeded   (proh-SEE-ded) continued onward, sometimes after a pause or interruption (page 10)